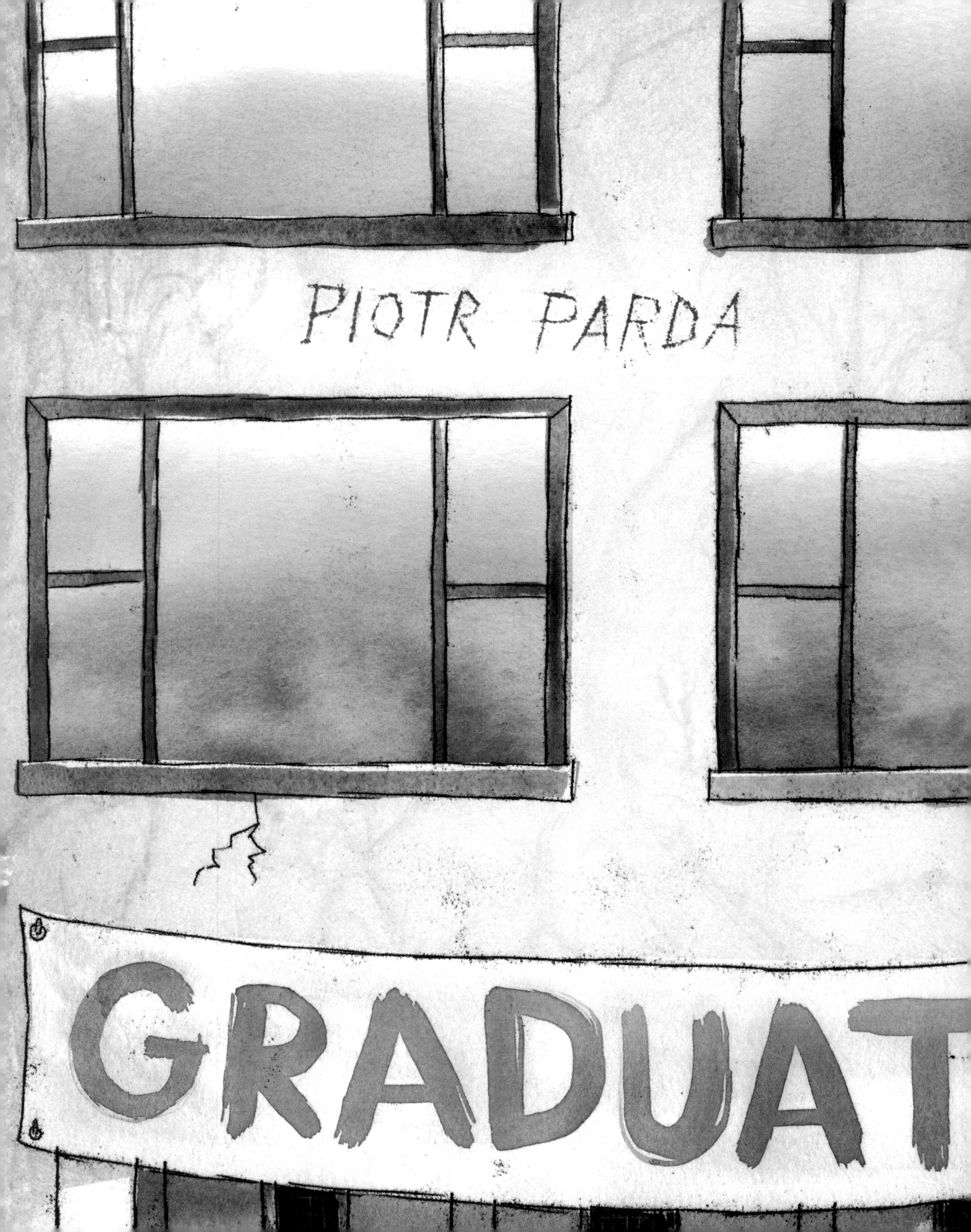
PIOTR PARDA
GRADUAT

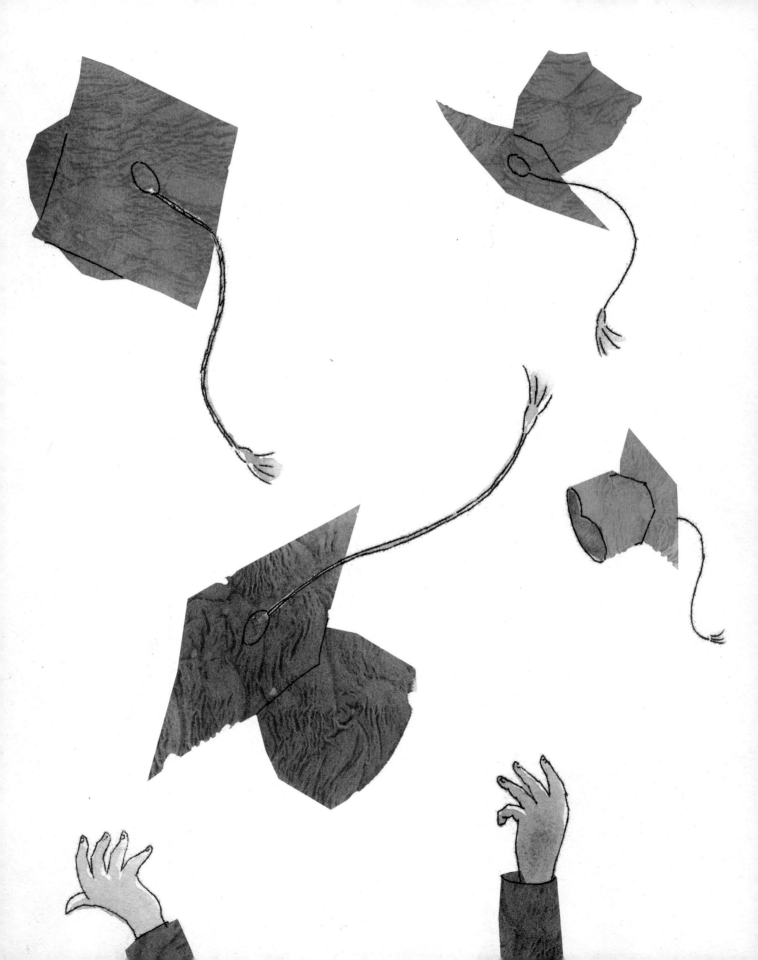

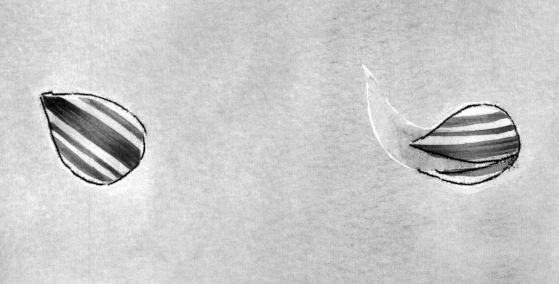

To Asia, Basia, and Emilka

First Edition 2017
Library of Congress Control Number 2016948538
ISBN 978-0-9913866-7-3

10 9 8 7 6 5 4 3 2 1
Printed in South Korea

The illustrations were done in watercolor and monoprint.
Book design by Piotr Parda

Ripple Grove
Press

Portland, OR
www.RippleGrovePress.com